Glow of Our Sweat

also by Francisco Aragón

Poetry

Puerta del Sol
Tertulia
In Praise of Cities
Light, Yogurt, Strawberry Milk

Translations

From the Other Side of Night
Sonnets to Madness and Other Misfortunes
Of Dark Love
Body in Flames
Lorca: Selected Verse (cotranslator)
Federico García Lorca: Collected Poems (cotranslator)

Editions

OCHO #15
The Wind Shifts: New Latino Poetry
Dánta: A Poetry Journal, #1 & 2
Mark My Words: Five Emerging Poets
Berkeley Poetry Review, #23/24

*For Rod —
Please accept
this modest*

Glow of Our Sweat

*volume as
a token of appreciation
for our lovely chat
the other evening —
New Year's Eve
2016/17*

Francisco Aragón

*3 January 2017
Torquay
Royal Pines*

Scapegoat Press
Kansas City, Missouri

Copyright © 2010 by Francisco Aragón

All rights reserved

Scapegoat Press
P.O. Box 410962
Kansas City, MO 64141
www.scapegoat-press.com

Cover art: "Glare" (2006) by Miguel Angel Reyes

"Glare" formed part of "Consejo Nacional de Talleres Portfolio, Creando Fuerzas"—an exhibit shown at Galería America at the Institute for Latino Studies at the University of Notre Dame from January 25 to March 9, 2007

Visit Miguel Angel Reyes's website at:
http://miguelangelreyes.com/

El poeta habla por teléfono con el amor by Frederico Garcia Lorca copyright © Herederos de Frederico Garcia Lorca. English Translation by Francisco Aragón, copyright © Francisco Aragón and Herederos de Frederico Garcia Lorca from Obras Completas (Galaxia/Gurenberg, 1996 edition). All rights reserved. For information regarding rights and permissions please contact lorca@artslaw.co.uk or William Peter Kosmas, Esq., 8 Franklin Square, London W14 9UU, England.

"VI" and "El otro día me encontré a Garcia Lorca" are reprinted with the generous permission of Francisco X. Alarcón.

Publisher's Cataloguing-in-Publication Data is available.

ISBN 978-0-9791291-3-1

This book is set in Californian FB and Impact. Californian FB is based on California Old Style, designed by Frederic W. Goudy for the University of California Press in 1938. Impact In 1958, Lanston issued it as Californian. Carol Twombly digitized the roman 30 years later for California; David Berlow revised it for Font Bureau with italic and small caps; Jane Patterson designed the bold. In 1999, assisted by Richard Lipton & Jill Pichotta, Berlow designed the black and the text and display series. Impact was designed by Geoffrey Lee in 1965 and released by the Stephenson Blake foundry.

In memory of John K. Walsh

mentor & friend

Contents

9   Author's note

      I

13   Love Poem
15   Torso
16   The Poet Speaks with His Beloved on the Telephone
17   The Slide
19   Gravel&Grass
21   In Secret
22   Symphony in Grey
24   Walt Whitman
25   Asleep You Become a Continent
26   Earplugs
27   Words In Space
30   Your Voice
31   Ars Poetica
33   San Francisco, 1985
35   The Tailor
37   To Madrid
38   Midtown Triptych
41   The Other Day I Ran Into García Lorca
42   Arttalk

      II

45   Flyer, Closet, Poem

59   Appendix (poems in Spanish)
65   Acknowledgements
66   Notes
72   About the Author

Author's Note

Poetry in conversation with prose. *In Praise of Cities* was my first attempt at it: a chapbook of poems punctuated by a prose meditation in the wake of September 11. I remember the freedom of it—the shunning, on my part, of any concern about what's expected, or what's the norm, in poetry publishing. Something similar is in play again. Writing the prose piece "Flyer, Closet, Poem" for the specific purpose of placing it here after these poems feels almost political—in the way that the personal can be political.

What distinguishes this effort from the *momotombito* chapbook of 2002 is that I've opted to include translations—new translations of poems I rendered years ago, but which fit, I think, into this book's arc. It's also the case that some of the poems are liberal versions or riffs inspired by other poets' poems, most of them originally in Spanish, and whose Spanish originals I include in an appendix. In this sense, the poet Maria Melendez, who followed the evolution of this manuscript, captured in an e-mail the spirit of what I was after: "[T]his inclusiveness affirms the Whitmanic view that, poetically, we are all a little bit of each other. It extends Blaser's open field across individual lives/minds/muses..." *Glow of Our Sweat*, more than a collection of poems, aspires to be a community of poems—multiple voices that mingle, converse, commiserate.

Human friend, let this poem hang in your brain upside down. Let it change us...

—*Maurice Kilwein Guevara*

But poems, like people, keep changing through time.

—*Gary Snyder*

he aprendido
a disimular
casi todo
pero
todavía
me delata
junto a ti
el desbocado
palpitar
de mi corazón

I

I've learned
to fake
nearly everything
but
still
when next to you
I'm given away
by the empty
pounding
of my heart

(Francisco X. Alarcón)

Love Poem

Just let the San Andreas
stay put, keeping this tunnel
intact, enough to amble

out of it, past *Louie's Dim
Sum* a Saturday afternoon,
a breeze detectable off

the bay—visible in the distance,
carrying with it the smells
of open air markets:

crab freshly caught
and seahorses piled
in bins along Stockton . . .

or Jack, strolling out of the tube
connecting Polk Gulch
and North Beach, on his way

to Aquatic Park to spread
the Sporting Green
on his favorite patch of grass...

He is ferrying the portable
radio to his ear,
listening for the count

in the bottom of the ninth
at Candlestick,
begins to smooth

the pages with his palms
before he sits
to keep it dry: the split

seat of his pants

for Jack Spicer (1925 – 1965)

Torso

Despite the absent head (whose eyes

were the green of apples)
the supple flesh hums
with the afterglow

of those eyes
which is why the curve
of chest shimmers which is why

the twist of loin turns
that look into a smile, snaring
your eyes, leading

them slowly to regions
below the waist...That block
of stone more than a figure

disfigured and short; cascade
of shoulder glints
like a sinewy beast

of prey, whose edges blink
like stars—that torso:
gazing on its own. Step closer:

go blind

after Rilke

The Poet Speaks with His Beloved on the Telephone

(Federico García Lorca)

Your voice watered the dune of my chest
in that sweet wooden booth.
South at my feet it was spring,
north near my face flowered a fern.

In that narrow space a radiant pine
sang, though with no seed nor dawn.
And my cry hung for the first time
a wreath of hope on the roof.

Sweet and faraway voice flowing for me.
Sweet and faraway voice tasted by me.
Faraway and sweet voice, muffled softly.

Faraway, like a dark wounded deer.
Sweet, like sobbing in the snow.
Faraway, sweet: lodged in the marrow!

The Slide

The twin concrete flumes
at Seward Park, just
below Kite Hill: knob

on the city's heart swaying
with fennel and grass;
and the one fir

jostling with the wind whipping
down from Twin Peaks.
The patchwork of the city

starts at my feet, reaching
the wide stitch of the bay,
and across it a friend

and his fever, his cough. Late
afternoons that July:
a bench, a view, the air

moving through the trees, men
trailing dogs out
for a piss, the smells.

And heading home one night
along a different path
I happen on those

companion slides, grassy slope
of that narrow
street park the base

of Kite Hill, secluded
between houses and pine—that space,
those years: adjusting

the sheets of wax paper
we'd tear off and slip
under us, perched and ready

at the top...then down
racing over the hump mid-way
and down again, spilling

over the lips of our chutes—
both of us in the end
sprawled in the sand.

Gravel & Grass

October had begun to show, ablaze
in the leaves of tree
after tree across the flat, scattered

campus near Bordeaux. Miko was up
against the trunk of an elm
explaining to Volker the key

to cutting the grapes on time.
And repeating to myself that day
I'll live in the south

of France the crunch underfoot
of gravel interrupted and filled
my ears and the smell

of cut grass my nose, shuttling
me across an ocean, a continent—
back I forget how many years

to the just-laid-down track
at State, tiers of eucalyptus
alongside the backstretch

of the 4-lap race I'd been training for
all spring. And I could almost
feel what I felt rounding

out of that final curve—acids
building in my legs
till calves and thighs flush

their waste, rinsing muscles
with pain, arms
stiffening, pupils starting to shift

from side to side as jerseys
left and right, pass me or fall
behind. You could have seen it

in my face: afternoons
that were my life then, what
coach said that first

session on the track...
...my frame clenched:
a pumping knot

rapidly approaching the wall

In Secret

What was it he felt
humming
beneath his skin? Gaze

of a twelve-year-old
feasting.
The hair on those arms.

Symphony in Grey
(Rubén Darío)

                Like glass

the color of mercury
it mirrors the sky's
sheet of zinc, the pale grey
a burnish splotched

with a flock of birds
while the sun's disc
like something injured crawls
slowly to the top

and the wind that blows
off the swells
dozes
in a trough,

its bugle a pillow.
Leaden waves crest
collapse—seeming
to groan near the docks

where he sits on thick
suspended rope,
smokes a pipe, his mind
sifting the sand in a faraway place.

An old wolf is what
he is. The light in Brazil
toasted his face. A strapping
storm from China

saw him tilt a flask of gin.
And foams laced
with salt, iodine
recall his curls, scorched

nose, his biceps
like those of an athlete,
his seaman's cap
and blouse. A screen

of tobacco smoke
lifts as did the fog
off the coast
that blazing noon

he set sail. Siesta
in the tropics. Our wolf
is nodding off—a grey
filming it all, as if the line

denoting the horizon
in a charcoal sketch
were to blur,
disappear. Siesta

in the tropics. Old cicada
is plucking its hoarse
forgetful guitar
while cricket draws

its bow across the one
string on its fiddle.

Walt Whitman

His country of iron where he lives: an older man, fatherly,
      strong, wholesome, calm,
his appearance impressive—the furrow of his brow
      persuades and charms, no end

to his soul that mimics a mirror, the tired curve of
      his shoulders draped with a cloak;
and with his harp—carved from oak—he sings his song
      like a prophet. He's a priest

fueling a wind that promises and promises...*Fly!*, he says
      to an eagle, to a seaman: *Row!*
while a chiselled, robust worker hears: *Put your shoulder*
      to the wheel! This is the path

our poet takes
—magnificent

face

            after Rubén Darío

Asleep You Become A Continent

(Francisco X. Alarcón)

asleep you become a continent—
undiscovered, mysterious, long,
your legs mountain ranges
encircling valleys, ravines

night slips past your eyelids,
your breath the swaying of the sea,
sprawled across the bed like
a dolphin washed ashore, your mouth

is the mouth of a sated volcano,
O fragrant timber, how *do* you burn?
you are so near, and yet so far

as you doze like a lily at my side,
I undo myself and invoke the moon—
I'm a dog watching over your sleep

Earplugs

Putty globes
thumbs press
into place;

drifting to sleep
beside you
for the first time,

trying to: your
seemingly distant
muffled snore

more than heard
—felt, at intervals;
and in between:

interior sound
of my breathing,
my heart.

Words in Space

standing on a chair
wearing nothing
but a shirt you begin

to recite Lucky's
speech aloud
punctuating

the night   we'd
descended those
added winding

stairs six doors down
from the JJ Centre
minutes from your office...

the Finance Minister
had made *his*
speech earlier in

the day keeping
you and your
staff busy

summarizing
in a pamphlet
for clients

till around ten
after which we
met at Flanagan's

for steak and beer
an hour or so
before your shirt

fell to the floor
before you
later put it

back on but I
prefer to dwell
on how

in the middle
of Lucky's rant
you begin to twitch

and rise
so that I approach
and slip

you in again
while the words
the tears the stains

the years the stones
leave your lips
floating

down   *so blue so calm*
each of them
beneath a little

translucent
parachute sweeping
into my ear

in that space
re-modeled Georgian
just off Parnell

Your Voice

Amazing the mood it's put me in.
And the sky's tint at this hour—out
on my own, occasional hum or zip

of a car, August the summer month
half the city splashes about
the Mediterranean, or north:

the beach at Donostia a jewel
—its Paseo the lip of a shell to walk.
It's hearing you what really pulls

me in, soft this interior punch,
recalling the sheen of your brow—we'd talk
with our limbs, the Liffey below, have lunch...

Re-lived this evening on the phone;
the pitch of your Dublin tone.

Madrid

Ars Poetica

> lock it up for nine full years,
> lock it up tight   —Horace

*He's trying to hide
a child too big to squeeze
into a cupboard...*

By the end we feel dread
for them—friar
and boy are led away

by soldiers while others
are rounded up in front
of the boarding school: one,

his only friend, looks on
intent, not knowing he's
laying his eyes on him

for the last time. He'll grow
to write, direct
Sarandon, Lancaster, Brooke

Shields as well as those from
his native France. *All
those films,* he said

*were studies—honing my skills
for the work
conceived that afternoon*

*when I was ten,
just before the end
of the war*

. . .

Or I could write: *The film
so moved him it left him*

speechless—*though he still
wanted to write about it, fill*

*pages. Days later he read
the piece where Malle said*

"*In any work of art
it's possible to start*

too soon."

San Francisco, 1985

It rolled past the Castro—
marquee big with NORTH

BY NORTHWEST—and slowed
to a stop. He was at the corner

outside *Twin Peaks*, spotting me near
the front facing out the door—the seats

reserved for the elderly, disabled
just behind the driver. Our eyes

met briefly before he turned
to his right to shout your name

across the busy street, yelled
that I was on this one,

for you to come back.
You'd begun the jog, the game

you both played—here comes
the 24 Divisadero:

Who will reach Alpine first:
you on foot, or him on wheels?

But this time you re-cross Market,
both of you boarding, the bus alive

with holiday shoppers, coursing
through the city. The three of us

exchange phrases the short ride
together and I almost don't say it

turning to him anyway:
How are you feeling?

You grin touching my sleeve.
So it's this. This is what stays,

what sticks to me. He left us
sooner than expected:

I never made it to Alta Bates.
Afraid, perhaps, I'd undo

a ride on MUNI one
December afternoon.

The Tailor

Church steps. Throng
off Piazza Navona craning
to glimpse bride and groom?
when above their heads rose

a woman on her back—stretcher
cresting
the crowd before running
aground at the wheels

of an ambulance—*she fainted*
you said, having read the look
on my face, *they've come to pay
last respects*...And so

months later at the "Filmo"
watching the dead
Italian star
in Rosselini's film, that day

re-starts: horse-drawn cart,
casket crushing
a bed of flowers: Aldo's
last stroll around

his parish, mourners trailing
behind as you did
in my thoughts
in the dark. You were out

of work, patterns for suits,
scissors, measuring
tape and chalk
in your sister's

closet. And what you took
the whole afternoon to say...
In the final scene
Fabrizi's hands are tied

behind his back
before his body is riddled
—a crumpled priest
slumped in a chair, firing

squad arrayed in a field
vast and abandoned as the square
we walked across that night, risen
from the checkered cloth:

pasta and half the wine
on your breath as we step
into the dark, heading for the road
that snakes behind

the Vatican leading to God
knows where—*a secret spot*
you say, *that not a soul
will find*...the moon

a perfect coin, ushering us
to the graves

To Madrid

July 20, 2005, Madrid

Little more than a six-letter word
on a globe for some twenty years

is what you were. And then I walked
hours and hours that

sweltering first day. In you
I have felt lonely and most

alive. From one of your cafés I hear
jackhammers, horns. Your pages

are open and spread on marble,
El País giving news of the living,

the dead: a first marriage (you're
suddenly the freest state

on earth); London burying her own.
That morning, a year ago,

waking to radio reports of your
mangled commuter-trains

a hint of what you are rose
in me. Calls, e-mails, calls.

More than any other
visit these years, I see

that you are not, really,
part of my past.

Midtown Triptych

    Broadway
past Lincoln
    Center and the wind

is up so seems
    to speak
saw you

    through the glass
standing in line
    I swear a quiver

played
    on your lips
you were

    leafing through his book...
—years
    it's been years

since Corona
    Heights, backing
into him: dribble,

    hook, swish...
...that beige
    comfy couch,

sipping a stem
    of wine, his cat
in my lap

• • •

The Townhouse
Saturday night—shoulder

to shoulder pushing
towards the piano he

stops to squeeze
by; his eyes mine

clench unclench...
...What was it we found

in common over
drink smoke talk?

A college campus
—his son, his daughter

• • •

Earlier that night I rose
to the city's surface
steam through the grate, crossed
crossed again down 7th

past Carnegie Hall, the greek
joint as imagined, chic
—unlike the shirt
D wore (the fur

of his arms) at Castro
and Market waiting
for the light: words were struck
like steel and flint

that distant August day...Then
his visit to Spain, mine
to New Canaan—walking
through the Morgan

with him. And what
our mouths unfurled
across a table of olives
years later—last night...

Dropping me off at 58th he
reaches for the door
I'm fumbling to open, leans
close and plants

what I've missed

all these years

The Other Day I Ran into García Lorca

(Francisco X. Alarcón)

I spotted him
the slim bow tie
those lips
those eyes
olive-colored

guitars wept
while the day
kicked
up its heels

abrupt
he stood
sauntered
straight
to my table

his mouth—
como sol
andaluz—
met my lips

Arttalk

Fuck
portraying
the sun's

   Why don't you paint

"petals of light."
Make something
darker, fun

   and shut your mouth

—the remains
of a moment:
glow of our sweat

   and I'll kiss it

                 after Jack Spicer (1925-1965)

II

Coming out is a process as endless as its audiences.

—*Kenji Yoshino*

Flyer, Closet, Poem

> This may sound strange, but I had no idea
> you were "family."
> —C. Dale Young

Someone hands me a flyer as I stride across the finish line. I slow to a walk, continue through the chute, gathering my breath as other promoters hand out flyers of their own. I roll them all into a paper baton. Next I head for the tables where volunteers are passing out T-shirts. Draping mine over my shoulder I scan and spot the large tents where refreshments are being served. Midway there, I unroll my squat tube and begin to look them over—each flyer a different color and vying for my attention: which race will I run next? The one I've just finished, the "Bridge to Bridge," covers eight miles along San Francisco's waterfront.

• • •

My first year in graduate school I read at a "pride" event. The organizer knew he could invite me: I'd had dinner with him—prompted by a mutual friend in another city, my former college roommate: the person "San Francisco, 1985" is addressed to. Days before the event, a fellow student who'd also been invited to read pulls me aside before class: "Francisco, do you mind if I announce our reading to the workshop?" In one sense, she is asking for permission to "out" me. We'd become friends early on and her question means she's correctly guessed that I'm shy about my sexual orientation. Although I easily consent to her announcement, it occurs to me that I had no intention of mentioning the reading at all.

• • •

Under a crisp autumn sky we lace up, jog in place, wait. At 9 A.M. the starting pistol sounds, releasing the vast throng gathered at the foot of Market in front of the Ferry Building—the Bay Bridge looming behind us. Runners, joggers and walkers stream along the Embarcadero and eventually through Fisherman's Wharf. After ascending a gentle slope, we crest over the top, coast towards Fort Mason, the Marina, along the Marina Green and across Crissy Field out to Fort Point—just below the south end of the Golden Gate Bridge. Think Vertigo: that scene in Hitchcock's film where Kim Novak intentionally falls into the bay, the water a frothy green—so that Jimmy Stewart can jump in to save her. *That* Fort Point. Once we reach it, we circle around an orange pylon and trek back—the tip of the Transamerica Pyramid and city skyline a distant view. We enter the chutes at the finish line, begin to collect flyers, head for the tents. All this on the grounds of the Presidio. The "Bridge to Bridge." It is—*was* my favorite race during those years when, as the end of "Gravel&Grass" suggests, running was my life.

• • •

Yale law professor Kenji Yoshino is on to something—vocabulary that perhaps describes my demeanor at UC Davis over ten years ago, and the years since. The following passage is from *Covering: The Hidden Assault on Our Civil Rights* (Random House, 2006):

> *Yet I did not know a word for this attempt to tone down my known gayness.*
>
> *Then I found my word, in sociologist Erving Goffman's book* Stigma. *Published in 1963, the book describes how*

> various groups—including the disabled, the elderly, and the obese—manage their "spoiled" identities. After discussing passing, Goffman observes that "persons who are ready to admit possession of a stigma...may nonetheless make a great effort to keep the stigma from looming large." He calls this behavior "covering."

Even though I'd been out to my mother since 1989; even though I'd written and published poems that could be deemed homoerotic; even though gay friends and mentors, including the late John K. Walsh, to whom *Glow of Our Sweat* is dedicated, had known I was gay: despite all of this, my sense is that I often lapse into certain patterns of behavior among people I assume are straight, including those I know to be gay-friendly.

In 1998, it took me over a year to come out to one particular mentor and friend in Davis, an Irish professor who made no secret of his and his wife's liberal views. What finally nudged me? I wanted to go to Ireland on a Fulbright and sought his advice. He promptly suggested a project: translating into Spanish the poems of one of Ireland's leading Irish-language poets who's also very openly gay. The proposal we put together prospered past the first round: the Fulbright committee in Washington, D.C. recommended it. In Ireland, though, it wasn't among the two projects finally selected for funding. Despite having come out to him, and despite our deepened friendship after this collaboration, I never shared with my professor-friend that among the reasons I'd applied for the grant, aside from my genuine interest in Irish poetry, was the fact that I was involved with someone in Dublin ("Earplugs," "Words in Space," "Your Voice"). Had this "someone" been a woman, I wonder if I would have remained silent.

. . .

When I was fifteen I ran a marathon. I'd joined the cross country team as a freshman to keep in shape for the upcoming basketball season. What I hadn't planned was the role running would come to occupy. Cross-country, track, road racing. These, and not basketball, became my principal pursuits. And also hitting the books. Like Richard Rodriguez, I became a "scholarship boy" in high school, was named valedictorian of my graduating class with acceptance letters from Stanford and UC Berkeley—the only schools I'd applied to. But also this: often in my gut a churning sensation. And in darker moments, this thought: *I'd rather be dead than have anyone, friend or stranger, learn my secret.*

And yet those years were mostly charmed. The straight A's, the athletic accomplishments—earning a varsity block as a sophomore; being active in student government; leading student retreats: all of these made up the intricate pieces of an attractive mosaic—but only on the surface. For beneath it all I never felt fully comfortable enough to seek out friends with whom I could be wholly myself—neither among peers, teachers, clergy, nor counselors. I was skilled at putting on a good front. But often, it was lonely.

One day a teacher I admire remarks that he's been to the Castro theater to see *Rear Window*. In the next breath—half-joking half-serious—he quips that after the movie ended and the lights came on, he filed up the center aisle, making sure to "clutch" onto his "visibly pregnant wife." Another teacher, the moderator of the Social Justice Club, once admits feeling "offended" whenever he sees two men kissing. And so...I keep my head buried in books, run laps around the track, mute certain feelings and thoughts.

Like Yoshino, I often wondered if I could "convert" and be normal. After I step onto the UC Berkeley campus, these beleagured thoughts eventually dissipate. Even from deep within the closet, self-acceptance seems possible. Yoshino says that upon reaching this stage—hidden self-acceptance—what we do is "pass." And when we're ready, if we're ever ready, we turn the knob, push open the door letting in some light, and step out. But even then, coming out of the closet can come to feel like a neverending hike. But the term that continues to needle me, and which largely describes my behavior more often than I care to admit, is "covering."

Not having the slightest intention of announcing to my fellow poets at UC Davis that I was taking part in a "pride" reading on campus was covering. Not reading the poems from section III of *Puerta del Sol* at my Notre Dame book launch in the spring of 2005, among colleagues, was covering. Not reading any of these "gay" poems at the ASU Kerr Cultural Center in Scottsdale, Arizona, in the spring of 2006 where, I'd been told, most attendees would be senior citizens, was covering.

And though I've appeared in a "gay" anthology, I've never, with any consistency, gone out of my way to identify as a "gay poet," nor as "a poet who happens to be gay." The C. Dale Young epigraph at the beginning of this essay is taken from a cordial Facebook message he sent me. In it he comments on a poem of mine ("Midtown Triptych") he read in a gay-themed, guest-edited journal where a poem of his also appears.

On the other hand, I've never been reticent about claiming

my status as "Latino poet." I've said many times that a Latino or Latina poet should be able to write however and whatever he or she wants and not feel any less "Latino" or "Latina" for it. I can't recall ever saying or writing that a gay poet should be able to do the same and not feel any less gay. In the former instance, the immutable trait—being Latino or Latina—can be considered, in my view, a source of pride. In the latter, the immutable trait—being gay or lesbian—is not so much a source of pride as something one accepts, yet downplays, or deftly omits from most conversations. This has been the case with me.

But why do I bring this up now? Why have I chosen to publish these nineteen poems and translations as a collection, and include this swath of prose, now? President Obama's lackluster leadership, thus far, on gay civil rights has prodded me to ask myself: And what role are you playing in this national conversation? I feel as if I can no longer remain quiet about who I am. I want to find ways to be more public in denouncing what is still, politically, a viable form of bigotry.

Which brings me to a story. It isn't about me but it very well could have been. It's a story about homophobia and poetry. It's the very anecdote that first led to gathering the poems and translations that form *Glow of Our Sweat* and, more pointedly, to write and include this essay. Ironically, it's a story I've opted to tell discreetly—using no names. By the end I think readers will see why.

Imagine a young man of nineteen. He's an articulate man who loves to read, who reads poetry and aspires to write. One of his favorite writers is an American poet born near the beginning of the 20th century, and who died when he was just over forty. In this he is not unlike the Spanish poet Federico García Lorca, who was born in 1898, and died at thirty-eight. Like Lorca, our American poet cultivated the sonnet. One commentator has described our American poet's sonnets as "darkly complex." One of these sonnets has snared our young man's imagination. It's a poem he's committed to memory, a poem whose literary allusions he's looked up, trying to better understand it. The young man, early on, admits to himself that he doesn't necessarily know what the sonnet means. But he loves it anyway. Over time, as he considers the circumstances of his own life—he is African American and gay—the poem begins to speak to him more deeply. It feels like an epiphany—that moment when he finds himself fully inhabiting the poem. It isn't anything in particular the sonnet says, but somehow he comes to feel that the author of the poem—also African American—experienced an isolation not unlike his own. Poem and reader become one. One day the young man is presented with the opportunity to share this poem, his relationship with this poem, on camera: it's a popular national initiative that allows people of all ages, backgrounds, levels of education, to recite a favorite poem and talk about it. The young man is selected to have a modest, but polished video produced, in which he'll get to share his passion for this poem. And he does, poignantly so. In some scenes, there is stained glass behind him. In another, he is seated in the pew of a church—for it happens that this young man's faith journey has been important to him. In still another scene, he is outdoors walking among trees. He shares his story, some parts of it sad—the derogatory remarks he has endured, the epithets, the feelings of isolation (he does indeed mention that he's gay). But the poem has been a refuge. Naturally, this American poet's heirs have given permission for their ancestor's sonnet to be a part of this national project. It is a well known poem, often anthologized, easy to find on the internet with a simple google search. For all practical purposes, it's in the public domain. What we imagine will be a formality—a copy of the video being sent to the esteemed American poet's heirs—turns out to be otherwise. The estate withdraws permission. The finished video cannot become part of the larger project and be disseminated. Apparently, the poet's estate is on firm legal ground. In essence, this African American poet's heirs are conveying to this articulate living young African American man: *We do not approve of who you are, what you are. We do not want your likeness, your voice, your name...associated with our esteemed ancestor.*

This story haunts me. The author of this famous sonnet, dead now since the mid-1940s, was a private man. He'd been married twice. I do not know what the rumor mills have said about his sexuality, but it reminds me of Federico García Lorca and the saga of his "Sonetos del amor oscuro"—an eleven-sonnet sequence addressed to the young man who was Lorca's great love, toward the end of his life. These were poems that were first introduced to me by my late mentor, John K. Walsh. Walsh eventually invited me to join him in co-translating them and they were subsequently published in 1991, shortly after my mentor died. I have included one of them ("The Poet Speaks with His Beloved on the Telephone") in *Glow of Our Sweat*.

For decades, after Lorca's death by firing squad, the existence of these sonnets is known in certain circles. Pirated editions circulate. But Lorca's heirs, apparently, resist having them officially published. Lorca's sexual orientation isn't something the family is eager to address or acknowledge. It isn't until 1984 that they allow the "Sonnets of Dark Love" to be published in the literary supplement of *ABC*, a newspaper in

Spain.

Are the heirs of our deceased African American poet in a similar frame of mind today, lest someone remotely suggest or suspect that their ancestor may have been gay?

...

Imagine another man—a boy, really, of fifteen. Here he comes, striding into the chutes at the finish line of the "Bridge to Bridge." You can see him walking towards a table to get his T-shirt before he continues to the refreshment tents. As he walks he's glancing over a bunch of flyers—handed to him and other runners. These flyers usually announce future local runs one can sign up for, races sponsored by local running clubs of various affinities and traits, sometimes benefiting this or that charity. He is not discarding any of them but places each one, after he's viewed it, at the bottom of the stack he'll take home to plan which races he'll run in the coming months. The flyers are of every color imaginable, with varying degrees of polish and design. The boy seems to be spending about ten seconds with each flyer, with no particular expression on his face, unless one considers the sheen of perspiration that's cooling his face. Wait. What's he doing with one of the flyers? It's a blue one and when he lays his eyes on it, scanning it with an expression we haven't seen before, he freezes in his tracks and looks up quickly, as if to monitor who might be watching him and in one swift motion, noticeable to no one, the flyer is air born—released from his fingers and floating to the ground. The expression on the boy's face seems a mixture of surprise and fear, as if he were concerned, again, about who might be watching him. Or an expression of pain: as if the paper the flyer were made of contained a secret acid that, when detecting dread in the person holding it, begins to release this acid into the pores of human skin, begins to burn the boy's very hand, its heat matching the dread in intensity. As if he has no choice but to rid himself of the flyer as humanly fast as possible—no time to simply walk it over to a nearby trashcan, scrunch it into a ball, and toss it in; or fold it quickly before stuffing it into the pocket of his running shorts—out of sight. But there it is, in plain sight, lying on the ground. Pick it up. What on earth does it say?

• • •

When I re-visit the poems in *Glow of Our Sweat*, some of which were begun years ago; when I re-live the process that resulted in "Flyer, Closet, Poem," I find myself wondering what shape, genre, and tone my writing will now take. Perhaps I've crossed a threshold of sorts. My poems have been described as quiet. Is it possible that in some of them I am covering? Or does understatement create room, space for readers to delve and explore, insert something of their own—their own voice, literally: the physical sound of it like an inner bridge that links, indelibly, a text to the person voicing it.

• • •

[...]

You could have seen it

in my face· afternoons
that were my life then, what
coach said that first

session on the track...
...my frame clenched:
a pumping knot

rapidly approaching the wall

June 2009
Washington, D.C.

Appendix

El poeta habla por teléfono con el amor

Tu voz regó la duna de mi pecho
en la dulce cabina de madera.
Por el sur de mis pies fue primavera
y al norte de mi frente flor de helecho.

Pino de luz por el espacio estrecho
cantó sin alborada y sementera
y mi llanto prendió por vez primera
coronas de esperanza por el techo.

Dulce y lejana voz por mí vertida,
dulce y lejana voz por mí gustada,
lejana y dulce voz amortecida,

lejana como oscura corza herida,
dulce como un sollozo en la nevada,
¡lejana y dulce, en tuétano metida!

(Federico García Lorca)

Sinfonía en gris mayor

El mar como un vasto cristal azogado
refleja la lámina de un cielo de zinc;
lejanas bandadas de pájaros manchan
el fondo bruñido de pálido gris.

El sol como un vidrio redondo y opaco
con paso de enfermo camina al cenit;
el viento marino descansa el la sombra
teniendo de almohada su negro clarín.

Las ondas que mueven su vientre de plomo
debajo del muelle parecen gemir.
Sentado en un cable, fumando su pipa,
está un marinero pensando en las playas
de un vago, lejano, brumoso país.

Es viejo ese lobo. Tostaron su cara
los rayos de fuego del sol del Brasil;
los recios tifones del mar de la China
le han visto bebiendo su frasco de gin.

La espuma impregnada de yodo y salitre
ha tiempo conoce su roja nariz,
sus crespos cabellos, sus bíceps de atleta,
su gorra de lona, su blusa de dril.

En medio del humo que forma el tabaco
ve el viejo el lejano, brumoso país,
adonde una tarde caliente y dorada
tendidas las velas partió el bergantín…

La siesta del trópico. El lobo se aduerme.
Ya todo lo envuelve la gama del gris.
Parece que un suave y enorme esfumino
del curvo horizonte borrara el confín.

La siesta del trópico. La vieja cigarra
ensaya su ronca guitarra senile,
y el grillo preludia un solo monótono
en la única cuerda que está en su violin.

(Rubén Darío)

Walt Whitman

En su país de hierro vive el gran viejo,
bello como un patriarca, sereno y santo.
Tiene en la arruga olímpica de su entrecejo
algo que impera y vence con noble encanto.

Su alma del infinito parece espejo;
son sus cansados hombros dignos del manto;
y con arpa labrada de un roble añejo
como un profeta nuevo canta su canto.

Sacerdote, que alienta soplo divino,
anuncia en el futuro, tiempo mejor.
Dice al águila: "¡Vuela!"; "¡Boga!", al marino,

y "¡Trabaja!", al robusto trabajador.
¡Así va ese poeta por su camino
con su soberbio rostro de emperador!

(Rubén Darío)

VI

al dormir te vuelves un continente,
largo, misterioso, sin descubrir.
tus piernas: cordilleras apartadas,
van circundando valles y cañadas

la noche se resbala por tus párpados,
tu respirar: vaivén de olas de mar,
en la cama te extiendes mansamente
como un delfín alojado en la playa

tu boca: boca de volcán saciado,
leño perfumado, ¿en qué fuego ardes?
estás tan cerca y a la vez, tan lejos

mientras duermes como lirio a mi lado,
yo me deshago, invoco a la luna:
ahora soy el perro guardian de tu sueño

(Francisco X. Alarcón)

El otro día me encontré a García Lorca

lo reconocí
por el moño
los labios
los ojos
olivos

lloraban
guitarras
y bailaba
flamenco
la tarde

de pronto
se paró
vino
directo
a mi mesa

y me plantó
un beso
como sol
andaluz
en mi boca

(Francisco X. Alarcón)

Acknowledgements

The poems in *Glow of Our Sweat*, often in earlier versions, have been previously published in journals and anthologies. I would like to gratefully acknowledge them here:

Beltway Poetry Quarterly (online): "Arttalk," "Symphony in Grey," "Torso"
Berkeley Poetry Review: "Arttalk," "San Francisco, 1985"
Chain: "Walt Whitman"
The Chattahoochee Review: "The Tailor," "Torso"
Dánta: "Symphony in Grey"
Electronic Poetry Review (online): "To Madrid"
Great River Review: "Ars Poetica"
Heliotrope: "Your Voice"
Jacket (online): "Love Poem,"
Mandorla: "Words in Space"
OCHO: "Midtown Triptych"
Tertulia (online): "Gravel&Grass"

"Arttalk," "Earplugs," "In Secret," "Torso," and "Your Voice" also appeared in *Mariposa: A Modern Anthology of Queer Latino Poetry* (Floricanto Press, 2008), edited by Emmanuel Xavier.

"Arttalk," and "Earplugs" also appeared in the anthology *Bend, Don't Shatter* (Soft Skull Press, 2004), edited by T. Cole Rachel and Rita D. Costello.

"The Slide" appeared in *How to Be This Man: The Walter Pavlich Memorial Anthology* (Swan Scythe Press, 2003)

"Asleep You Become a Continent" previously appeared (as sonnet "VI") in *Of Dark Love* (Moving Parts Press, 1991) and *The Other Side of Night: New and Selected Poems* by Francisco X. Alarcón (University of Arizona Press, 2002)

"The Poet Speaks with His Beloved On the Telephone" appeared in *Federico Garcia Lorca: Collected Poems* (Farrar, Straus & Giroux, 1991)

"The Other Day I Ran Into García Lorca" appeared in *Body In Flames* (Chronicle Books, 1990), and in *The Other Side of Night: New and Selected Poems* by Francisco X. Alarcón (University of Arizona Press, 2002)

I would like to thank Ben Furnish at Scapegoat Press for making this book possible; Miguel Angel Reyes, for consenting to use "Glare" as the cover of this book; John Matthias, who instilled in me the notion that other texts can provide vital starting points for new poems and versions; María Meléndez and Fred Arroyo for valuable feedback on the manuscript; Sandra McPherson, whose graduate seminar on Love and Desire first gave me the idea, over ten years ago, of perhaps attempting a collection like *Glow of Our Sweat*; Francisco X. Alarcón, mentor and friend whose own work and life have been an inspiration over the years; Billy Bussell Thompson, for helping keep alive my and others' memories of John K. Walsh. Special thanks to the Ragdale Foundation for a residency in the spring of 2009, during which I found an order to, and tinkered with, these poems, and also where the first draft of "Flyer, Closet, Poem" was written; the Institute for Latino Studies at the University of Notre Dame, for allowing me to benefit from artist residencies.

A heartfelt thanks to the Macondo Writers Workshop in San Antonio, Texas, the Guild Complex in Chicago, Illinois, and the Latino Writers Collective in Kansas City, Missouri—communities who have, in their own unique ways, supported and nourished me these past few years. Thanks, as well, to those friends and writers who have welcomed me to Washington, D.C., my new hub.

Notes

Love Poem

The "San Andreas" is the San Andreas Fault, which runs 800 miles through California. *The San Francisco Chronicle*, a daily newspaper, had a sports section whose pages used to be green and was commonly referred to as "The Sporting Green." "Candlestick" is a reference to Candlestick Park, a sports stadium located at Candlestick Point on the western shore of the San Francisco Bay. The San Francisco Giants used to play their baseball games there. The second half of this poem is largely inspired by having read *Poet, Be Like God: Jack Spicer and the San Francisco Renaissance* (Wesleyan University Press, 1998), a biography by Lewis Ellingham and Kevin Killian, which I read while in a seminar on the San Francisco Renaissance conducted by Gary Snyder at UC Davis.

Torso

This poem is inspired by Rilke's famous sonnet, "Torso of an Archaic Apollo." My version attempts a different ending ("Go blind") from the original ("You must change your life.")

The Poet Speaks with His Beloved on the Telephone

This is a new translation of the Lorca sonnet, "El poeta habla por teléfono con el amor," which forms part of the series, "Sonnets of Dark Love." The previous version, a co-translation with the late John K. Walsh, appeared in *Federico Garcia Lorca: Collected Poems* (Farrar, Straus & Giroux, 1991)

The Slide

For the record, for *my* record, "the friend" who's contending with "his fever, his cough" in the middle of the poem is the late John. K. Walsh.

 Gravel&Grass

The "just-laid-down track at State" refers to the track and field facilities at San Francisco State University, where the league track and field finals, when I was in high school, were sometimes held.

 Symphony in Grey

This is a relatively liberal translation or version of Rubén Darío's poem, "Sinfonía en gris mayor."

 Walt Whitman

This is a very liberal version or riff of Rubén Darío's traditional sonnet, also titled "Walt Whitman," from his ground-breaking collection *Azul*, published in 1888, a volume that included both poetry and prose.

 Asleep You Become a Continent

This is a new translation of Francisco X. Alarcón's sonnet, which previously appeared as "VI" in his fourteen sonnet sequence (with line drawings by Ray Rice) that made up *De Amor Oscuro / Of Dark Love* (Moving Parts Press, 1991), translated by Francisco Aragón

 Words In Space

"Lucky" is a reference to Samuel Beckett's signature character in, Waiting for Godot, in which, near the end, he delivers his famous stream-of-consciousness speech / rant. The "JJ Centre" is a reference to The James Joyce Centre at 31 North Saint George's Street, Dublin 1, in Ireland.

Your Voice

In the month of August in Spain, especially in the big cities, it's common for people to take one month of vacation and head to any of Spain's coastal towns or resorts. "Donostia" is the Basque spelling for "San Sebastian," the coastal town in the Basque Country in the north of Spain. This sonnet's rhyme scheme is borrowed from Robert Pinsky's "Sonnet."

Ars Poetica

The film being depicted in the first part of the poem is Louis Malle's *Au revoir les enfants*, which premiered in 1987. It is based on Louis Malle's experience as a ten year old boy during the second world war, the trauma of seeing his young Jewish friend being taken away and who, unbeknownst to him at the time, perished in a concentration camp. The italicized passages represent sentiments expressed by Malle in an interview I read in the Spanish press shortly after the film was released, including the sentiment expressed in the second part of the poem.

San Francisco, 1985

This poem is addressed to David Glidden, one of my roommates at Le Chateau Residence Club in Berkeley, CA, during the three years I lived there while an undergraduate at UC Berkeley. David's partner, Daniel Alferi, who passed away from AIDS early in the epidemic, is the other character in the poem.

The Tailor

The great Italian actor, Aldo Fabrizi, died in Rome on April 2, 1990. I stumbled upon his funeral. The "Filmo" is a reference to "La Filmoteca" in Madrid—a refurbished classical movie house that shows a plethora of old classic films from various countries and traditions, in their original language. The film mentioned in the poem is Roberto Rossellini's classic, *Rome, Open City*, filmed in Rome in 1945, depicting occupied Rome in 1944. Aldo Fabrizi plays a Roman Catholic priest who is executed by firing squad for refusing to collaborate with the Nazis. The "square" near the end is Saint Peter's Square in front of Saint Peter's Basilica in Vatican City.

To Madrid

Same-sex marriage became legal in Spain on July 3, 2005. In addition to legalizing same-sex marriage, Spain also legalized the adoption of children by same-sex couples, thereby surpassing the Netherlands and Belgium in rights afforded to the gay population, making Spain, in essence, the country in the world that afforded the most rights to its GLBT population. On July 20, 2005, *El País*, a Spanish national daily published a story about the first gay marriage in Madrid, as well as a story about memorial services being held in London: on July 7, 2005, four suicide bombers claimed the lives of 52 people and injured 700 in the capital of England.

On March 11, 2004 a series of coordinated bombings on commuter trains heading for the Atocha train station in Madrid claimed the lives of 191 people and wounded 1,800. The conservative Popular Party's handling of the crisis in the days that followed, in which they insisted that the bombings had been carried out by Basque terrorists, despite the mounting evidence that they weren't, coupled with the Popular Party's support of Bush's war in Iraq, which was overwhelmingly unpopular, caused the Socialist Party to be voted back into power on March 14, 2004.

Midtown Triptych

Part I: the book being "leafed through" is the *Strange Hours Travel-*

ers Keep (Farrar, Straus & Giroux, 2004) by August Kleinzahler. "Corona Heights" is a reference to Corona Heights Park near the Haight-Ashbury District of San Francisco. There are basketball courts there where, many years ago, I used to play one-on-one basketball.

Part II: The Townhouse is a gay bar at 236 East 58th Street in New York City.

Part III: "the Morgan" is a reference to The Morgan Library & Museum at 225 Madison Avenue in New York City.

The Other Day I Ran Into Garcia Lorca

This is a new translation of Francisco X. Alarcón's poem, "El otro día me encontré a García Lorca," which previously appeared in *Cuerpo en llamas / Body in Flames* (Chronicle Books, 1990), translated by Francisco Aragon

Arttalk

The text in italics are lines from Jack Spicer's poetry.

Flyer, Closet, Poem

Epigraph:
The poet C. Dale Young is the author of *The Day Underneath the Day* (Northwestern University Press, 2001, *Second Person* (Four Way Books, 2007) and the forthcoming *Torn* (Four Way Books, 2012). He blogs at: http://avoidmuse.blogspot.com/

The Castro theater is an old classic movie house located in the heart of the Castro District in San Francisco.

About the Author

A native of San Francisco and a former long-term resident of Spain, Francisco Aragón is the author of *Puerta del Sol* (Bilingual Press) and editor of the award-winning, *The Wind Shifts: New Latino Poetry* (University of Arizona Press). His work has appeared in a range of anthologies, including *Inventions of Farewell: A Book of Elegies* (W.W. Norton), *American Diaspora: Poetry of Displacement* (University of Iowa Press), *Evensong: Contemporary American Poets on Spirituality* (Bottom Dog Press), *Deep Travel: Contemporary American Poets Abroad* (Ninebark Press) and, most recently, *Mariposa: A Modern Anthology of Queer Latino Poetry* (Floricanto Press). His poems and translations (from the Spanish) have appeared in various print and web publications, including, *Chain, Crab Orchard Review, Chelsea, The Journal*, the online venues, *Jacket, Electronic Poetry Review*, and *Poetry Daily*. He directs Letras Latinas, the literary program of the Institute for Latino Studies at the University of Notre Dame. He is also the editor of Canto Cosas, a book series from Bilingual Press featuring the work of Latino and Latina poets. He is a member of the Macondo Writing Workshop in San Antonio and on the board of the Association of Writers and Writing Programs (AWP). Visit his website at: http://franciscoaragon.net.